I0636385

Christopher Pearse Cranch

Kobboltozo

A Sequel to the Last of the Huggermuggers

Christopher Pearse Cranch

Kobboltozo
A Sequel to the Last of the Huggermuggers

ISBN/EAN: 9783337109417

Printed in Europe, USA, Canada, Australia, Japan

Cover: Foto ©Andreas Hilbeck / pixelio.de

More available books at **www.hansebooks.com**

WITH ILLUSTRATIONS

BY

CHRISTOPHER PEARSE CRANCH

BOSTON 1889

LEE AND SHEPARD Publishers

10 Milk St. next "The Old South Meeting House"

NEW YORK CHARLES T. DILLINGHAM

718 and 720 Broadway

CONTENTS.

KOBBOLTOZO.

CHAPTER ONE.

INTRODUCTION.

INCE the publication of The Last of the Huggermuggers, I have received a letter from Mark Scrawler, Esq., who dates from the town of Aristides, Ohio, in which he professes to be very angry that I have published my little story about the giant, particularly as he (who was engaged by Mr. Nabbum to write a full account of every thing) was not even consulted in the case. Mr. Scrawler makes a long letter of it. He complains that his rights have been infringed upon: that he had taken a great deal of trouble in accumulating and arranging his facts, having made copious notes of all that occurred in the giant's island, as well as during the voyage homeward, interspersed with reflections of his own — including some valuable observations on the probable origin of the Huggermugger race, as well as the results of his investigations into shell-fish of the conch and of the bivalve species. "His work," he says, "was progressing slowly on account of the magnitude of his subject. It would have been one of the most valuable scientific works of the day.

Mr. Scrawler laughs to scorn our slender juvenile publication, which he stigmatizes as "a penny-trumpet affair — a cobweb to catch flies — a flimsy, childish, weak, uncalled-for, not-to-be-thought-of-for-a-moment tissue of absurdities." "Why," he exclaims, "bring out these great scientific facts in the light form of a story-book for children? The sensible Bostonians, New Yorkers, Philadelphians, and all the sensible American citizens in general, demand more solid food. Has, for instance, anything been said in this gilded child's-rattle of a book, of the geology or botany of the giant's island — of the height and breadth of Huggermugger and his wife — of the shape and dimensions of Huggermugger Hall — of Huggermugger's farm-yard — of the vegetables, the fruits, the bread, the meat, the frogs, the fish, and especially of the enormous and singular 'clams' which formed his daily food? Or of the clothes the giants wore, how they were obtained, of what stuff they were woven — and who were Huggermugger's tailors, who his hatters, who his suspender-makers, who taught him English, who supplied him with tobacco, and pipes, and ale? Or has anything been said of the community of dwarfs, of their habits, size, appearance, language, &c., &c.? What presumption," he adds, "for any one to come before the public, (were it only the juvenile public) with such a lame, one-sided, pitiful statement of facts, with nothing to recommend them but the clap-trap trickery and varnish of the story form. The whole thing," he says, "is unworthy a man of sense and thought."

Mr. Scrawler intimates that, of course, *he* would have given a very different title to *his* book, and would have shone resplendent on the title-page with a very choice and appropriate motto from Shakspeare — in the following style : —

> " Why man, he doth bestride the narrow world
>   Like a Colossus, and we petty men
>   Walk under his huge legs " —

after which some *stars* — and then

> *" Upon what meat doth this our Cæsar feed,*
> *That he is grown so great ? "*

" Compare a title-page with such a quotation upon
it — flaming (he adds with a preternatural poetical fer-
vor,) flaming ' like a star in the forehead of the
morning ' — compare it with the plain, methodistical
style in which you have decked the vacant brow of
your weak bantling ! "

Mr. Scrawler goes on in this vein, boastful of himself and vituperative of us, and concludes with vaguely
hinting at a lawsuit.

In our little story we briefly stated our reasons, in
a note, for proceeding to print our account. Some
years had elapsed, and Mr. Scrawler's work had not
appeared. We heard also, from pretty good authority,
that he had shown portions of his book, as far as it
was written, to several publishers, who threw buckets
of cold water upon his ardent hopes, and not only
declined to publish such " solid " — they even said
" heavy " — writing, but advised him outright to dis-
continue it, and take to something else for a living.

We have also been scolded and threatened in
another quarter. Mr. Alonzo Scratchaway, the artist

who accompanied the Nabbum expedition, threatens to
indict us for stealing his illustrations and spoiling
them. He says he intended to have brought out a
folio edition (as big as Audubon's Birds) of colored
lithograph Huggermugger illustrations, designed to ac-
company Scrawler's work, as an atlas accompanies a
geography — " and he'll do it yet, whether Scrawler
publishes or not. None of your petty wood-cuts,"
says Scratchaway, " but something as grand and original as Retsch, or Flaxman, or Gustave Doré."

Here I believe we get to the end of our troubles
on the score of our (as we thought) inoffensive little
book. We believe that Mr. Zebedee Nabbum has not
yet complained of misrepresentation as to his charac-
ter or dialect; that Little Jacket (or Mr. John Cable)
does not look otherwise than favorably on our narrative of his curious adventures, and that Mr. Barnum
is above imputing any ill feeling in the allusions we
have made to his name.

CHAPTER TWO.

TWO OLD COMRADES GO OFF TOGETHER.

PRESUMING that our young readers are acquainted with the giants' story alluded to in the foregoing chapter, I will now proceed to give a narrative of what occurred in the island, after the departure thence of Huggermugger and the American sailors — and I will state before I am through, how I came to obtain my information.

The reader will recollect that it was thought by some that Little Jacket (or John Cable, as he has for some time been called) went out West, and settled down as a farmer : while it was reported by others that he was still cruising with Mr. Nabbum in search of the wonderful. There is a basis of truth in both accounts. John Cable went out West, and thinking himself tired of a sea life, turned farmer for a while, during which he grew to be a good deal stouter and taller. But the old love of sea life returned, and he gave up farming, and came to New York to see what advantageous employment might be found on board some good ship. Here it chanced that he fell in once more with his old comrade, Nabbum, who was just about making another voyage of discovery. The long and the short of it is, that Jacky Cable and Zebby Nabbum sailed together, secretly intending to visit once more the giant's island.

There were no particular incidents worth noting on board ship. The voyage was a pretty long one. I believe they touched at the Cape of Good Hope and the Island of Madagascar. At last the island of the giants loomed in the distance.

As they drew near the coast, Zebedee sighed to think what a great speculation failed when Hugger-mugger died. Jacky, too, sighed, but it was to think how lonely it would be there now, and how changed, since the good giant and giantess were no more. Now, they should see no one but the dwarfs, with the spiteful Kobboltozo perhaps made king of the island.

They determined, however, to travel into the in-
terior of the island, and to ascertain how things had
gone on since their departure. Having cast anchor in
a secure bay, Nabbum and Jacky went ashore in a
boat, and landed near the well-known beach where
the great shells were. They took with them pro-
visions for several days' journey, and proceeded by
the nearest road towards Huggermugger Hall and the
neighboring village of the dwarfs. They encountered
the usual difficulties in clambering over the great
rocks and pushing their way through the tall shrubs
and weeds. They found, too, many things to wonder
at, which they did not recollect having noticed before.
High over their heads waved great palms and mag-
nolia trees—enormous grasshoppers sprang by them—
gigantic butterflies flashed overhead, their wings blazing with purple and gold. Birds as big as eagles
darted from tree to tree, singing as loud as hand-
organs, and filling the trackless woods with their strange
jargon. Nabbum compared it to an immense giant
menagerie, and Jacky said it reminded him of some
monster concert about to commence, when from the
double basses up to the octave flutes, all the musicians
in the orchestra were running up and down the scales

on their instruments, and all the people in the pit talking at the top of their voices at the same time. Then there were huge flowers that flaunted over their heads, loading the air with thick perfume—some like banners, scarlet, orange, and blue—some that hung their bells, like great church-bells, which even seemed to be vibrating sometimes with a low ringing, weighed down and swinging with the weight of the enormous bees that hummed inside with their bagpipe drone. Now they would pass near a marsh, where the frogs were plunging in their noontide bath, or croaking with voices like young bull-calves. Now their way lay near enormous ravines which one might fancy the favorite haunts of the boa-constrictor and rattle-snake—but there were no poisonous reptiles in the island, for the Hug-germugger race (like St. Patrick) had long since exterminated them—and now they would climb a hill, from which they could see afar the top of Huggermugger Hall, looming like an enchanted castle. Ah! there was no Huggermugger to take them there in his basket—no Mrs. Huggermugger to welcome them to her hospitable dwelling.

CHAPTER THREE.

MESSRS. NABBUM AND CABLE FIND THINGS CHANGED IN THE GIANT'S ISLAND.

FTER a rather fatiguing tramp, our two travellers reached the deserted mansion. On approaching, they saw that the front door was wide open. They at once suspected that Kobboltozo, or some of the dwarfs were there, and had taken possession of the house. Perhaps they had made havoc of all that the giant had left behind him. They ascended the stairs, but saw no one. There was little change since they had left. But how dreary seemed the great mansion, without the good host and hostess who had once entertained them there! There was something very desolate in such a great house being forevermore untenanted. There stood the two great arm-chairs at either side of the huge chimney, and on the mantel-piece there was still the great shell in which Jacky was brought to the giant's house. There was the table at which the giant and giantess had sat. There was the bed where Mrs. Huggermugger had died. There were her huge scissors, and knitting-needles, and dis-taff—there even her dresses hanging on the wall. There were the old boots that had waded through the marshes, and the old fish-basket that had brought home so many muscles,* and oysters, and clams. And high above all was the great window—like an immense studio-window, pouring down a flood of light upon all. Now the Huggermugger's tramp-tramp was no more heard through the corridors—the wreaths of curling pipe-smoke no more arose to the rafters—the great voices no more came rumbling from room to room—the uproarious laughter was forever silent.

Our visitors roamed about the house with mingled

---

* A friend suggests that it was probably a species of *muscle* on which our giant friends fed, which naturally might have contributed to the increase of their limbs. Another suggests that in their religious creed they might have been *mussulmen*. But I think my friends were joking.

feelings of curiosity and sadness. They expected
every moment to meet some of the dwarfs, but found
no traces of any living being. All was silent as the
grave. Now and then the chirp of a solitary cricket
resounded under the desolate hearthstone, like the
shrill noise of some one filing. A melancholy big
robin sang in the neglected garden outside, and it
seemed like a requiem over the departed ; and overhead they heard the long wail of the locust, swelling
and dying like a bell through the still summer air.
Every thing within and without was desolate, deserted,
neglected. But there were signs of some one's having
been there since their departure. Not only was the
outer door found open, but the floor of the great hall
was scattered over here and there with fragments as
of a feast, — plates. dishes, bottles, and dry scraps of
food were found, which had evidently belonged to the
dwarfs, and on the hearth were the remains of half-
burnt brands, and cooking utensils of much too dimin-
utive a pattern to have served the giants.

Our two adventurers left the giant's house, and
proceeded towards the village of the dwarfs, expecting
every moment to meet some one who would give
them some information of what had passed. But they

saw no one. They reached at length the village, but
found all deserted — not the trace of a living creature.
The houses were all forlorn and neglected — some of

them without doors, or windows, or chimneys — the
fences half fallen, the gate-hinges rusty and broken,
great burdocks and thorn-apples and other rank weeds
of enormous size growing over and almost conceal-
ing them, and every thing evincing the most utter
desolation. They went up and down, searching in
vain for some living being. They called, but no one
answered. At last they saw some one appear at the
door of one of the huts, peeping timidly out, and a

wan little * figure appeared and came out to meet them.

This little figure was the dwarf Stitchkin, the tailor. Our friends remembered him, though they did not at first recognize him. This little tailor had been sometimes employed to make Huggermugger's clothes; but having been obliged to look up to such a height when he measured the giant, he always foreshortened his figure, and consequently made his coats excessively short in the waist : so that Mrs. H. persuaded her husband to employ him no longer, at least to make his coats. The little man seemed glad to see our friends back again. When questioned about the disappearance of the rest of the dwarfs, and the dilapidated state of their village. the tailor sighed and said: "My friends. it is my belief that they are all gone — dead or lost — and that I am the only survivor of the dwarfs."

"And Kobboltozo." said Jacky, "what has become of him ?"

"I know not." said Stitchkin. " and yet — it is a

* It must be remembered that we measure by the giant scale. We call the dwarfs little, because they were so in comparison with Huggermugger.

long story and very singular one. If you wish, you
shall hear it. But come. let us leave this wretched
place, and seat ourselves under yonder great tree :
and there, in the cool shade. I will tell you all I
know of the history of Kobboltozo and the other of
my race."

So the three went and seated themselves on the
grass under the trees. and after Mr. Nabbum had
treated the tailor to some luncheon, out of the pro-
visions he had brought with him from the ship. and
refreshed him with a bottle of good ale, Stitchkin
gave the narrative from which we compile the following singular history.

CHAPTER FOUR.

HOW KOBBOLTOZO BORE THE GIANT'S DEPARTURE.

KNOW (said Stitchkin) that we small people are looked upon by you foreigners as a hard-natured, selfish race of beings. I think it must be true, for none of my tribe ever did *me* any kindness that I know of, and I have always found it very difficult to live among them. I was somehow different from them all. I made clothes for them, but half the time they didn't pay me; so that I was poor and oppressed, and lonely, while those around me were flourishing and happy.

But none of them were as bad as Kobboltozo. He never was liked by any of us. I dare say you know that he was the cause of Huggermugger's misfortunes

and departure. When the giant went away in your
ship, he could not repress his joy.

He had watched with malicious
delight the preparations making for
Huggermugger's departure. He sat
on a rock, from which he saw the
giant go aboard the ship. He saw
the sailors receive him on deck —
he saw them hoist their sails, and
lingered till the ship was out of
sight. He then snapped his fingers,
grinned with satisfaction, stood up,
danced, and sang a snatch of bar-
barous melody.

" Aha!" he said, " Old Hugg, you
are safe now. *You'll* never come
back — *you* will never arrive at the country of these
foolish sailors — you'll die on board, and they'll chuck
you overboard, and give your great carcass to the
sharks. *Your* fate is settled, I think. Hurrah ! The
dwarfs, as you called us, will be kings of the island ;
and who knows but some of us may yet grow to be
as great as the Huggermuggers ! "

So saying, Kobboltozo almost turned a summerset

in his delight. Returning homeward, he met some of his friends, and told them they had seen the last of Huggermugger. They knew that the giant had gone, and were in as great glee as the shoemaker.

"Come," said Kobboltozo, "what shall we do? suppose we have a great feast, and a carouse?"

"Agreed!" cried the dwarfs. "Let's go and summon all our neighbors, and their wives and children, and tell the good news — that the giant has gone, and the island is ours. Then for the feast — where shall it be? where shall it be?"

"Suppose we have it in Huggermugger Hall," said Kobboltozo.

"Agreed!" said they all. And there was a general scrambling and tumbling over the great rocks and stones, and a plunging through the bushes: and while some ran to summon their neighbors, others made their way to the giant's house, and crowded up to the door. To their great disappointment, however, they found it shut and locked. Whereupon ensued a tremendous hubbub. Some swore, others banged with their sticks, others brought stones and tried to batter the door, others proposed to set fire to it. At last Keholo, the locksmith, thought he could pick the lock.

So they brought a ladder and placed it against the huge portal, and Keholo mounted with the biggest instruments he could procure for the purpose. The crowd was very impatient, but in the course of an hour the huge fastening, which was of simple construction, (for Huggermugger being perfectly unsuspicious and fearless of the dwarfs, never thought a complicated lock necessary, and in fact seldom locked his door at all, but kept open house to all,) gave

way—and the door, with the crowd all pressing at once against it, slowly opened. In rushed the crowd, and up the great stone steps they mounted—they

were accustomed to climbing — and entered the great
hall. The solemn silence of the place would have
been oppressive to any but these hard-natured beings ;
and indeed there were some among them who felt
it — some who had looked up to the giant with awe
and respect, even with admiration — some who, if they
did not love, at least did not hate him — some who
had had good reason to remember him as a protector
and benefactor. These felt ill at ease in this great
house. What right had they to be there? How could
Huggermugger's departure benefit them? — and why
should they assemble here — why hold here a feast to
celebrate the absence of the rightful lord and pro-
prietor of the domain — of him to whom this house,
this whole island was fitted, far better than for
them ?

However, as is usual in such cases, the majority
overruled the minority, and the few who at first felt
a reluctance to join the mob, soon found themselves
carried along with the multitude in the excitement of
the occasion.

CHAPTER FIVE.

THE FEAST OF THE DWARFS.

 AVING dragged up stairs the ladder. the dwarfs bore it with them into the great hall. and raised it against the table, which stood in the centre of the room. There was great talking and shouting and laughing as they mounted the table, and capered to and fro upon it.

"Ha, ha!" they cried, "only think of it — the giant's house is ours — the island is ours — the dwarfs are kings of the land — every thing is ours! Hurrah! Quick — let us have our feast here. on this very table — ere sundown!"

So while some ran out to bring bread and meat, and fish and vegetables. and fruits and plates, and knives and forks. and spoons and tumblers, others dragged out one of the giant's saucepans, and lit a fire on the hearth, and began preparations for cook-

ing. All found something to do. The women were as active as the men. Whatever they could fetch ready-cooked from their houses, they brought ; and whatever could serve them in the giant's house. they unscrupulously used. What chiefly delighted them was the discovery of some bottles of ale. and also a half empty beer-barrel, which they contrived to tap and set its contents flowing. The bottles they could not so easily manage. as they were very tightly corked.

When the feast was ready, they all mounted upon the table. and seated themselves at the banquet. Kobboltozo, as president, opened the feast with a speech. in which he congratulated his friends on the

departure of Huggermugger, and the possession of the
giant's house and island by the dwarfs.

"Friends," he said, "let us hail with joy this
auspicious day. He who once lorded it over us, the
giant whom we feared — he who by reason of his
tremendous size could not fail to be a tyrant over us
smaller people, has gone — gone forever, let us hope,
and the island belongs to us. Now we are all free
and equal. No one can say, 'I am greater than my
neighbor.' Every one is at liberty to act as he pleases.
What doubt is there that we shall now prosper in our
affairs, and all grow rich — all grow powerful?

"Friends, I propose a toast: 'Hurra for liberty and
equality, and each man for himself.'"

So they all fell to eating and drinking. There was
great merriment and noise. Pretty soon the strong
giant-beer got into their heads, and the feast became
a wild orgy. They shouted, they laughed, they em-
braced, they stood up, they danced, they turned sum-
mersets among the plates and glasses, they quarrelled
and pelted each other—nothing could exceed the wild
reckless extravagance of this feast.

Presently some one proposed to drink Huggermugger's health, in a bottle of his own ale. There was

a general roar of assent. "What a capital idea — ha, ha! drink the giant's health and a long voyage to his highness! — drink his health in his own ale — ha, ha! *He'll* never drink it again. Come, some of you, help me get this big bottle on the table! yo-heave-o! — once more! up with him — there! But how shall we get the cork out? Can anybody find Huggermugger's corkscrew?"

"O, but don't you see," said another, "its only fastened in with ropes. Here, bring your hatchet, Hammawhaxo!" and the carpenter soon cut the ropes

which held the huge cork. But the dwarfs did not know what frisky ale this was — for no sooner were the fastenings cut, than fz—z—zzzf fzFFFZZ—POPP!!!! out flew the cork into their faces, knocking over some half dozen of them, who lay insensible for some time,

and out foamed the frothy ale, deluging and nearly
drowning a half dozen more, wetting nearly every
one from head to foot, and streaming in torrents down
from the table.

This unlucky adventure rather sobered the company
for a while, and they concluded to let the other bottles alone.

One foolish fellow, however, who had drank quite
enough, and who had left the festive scene to take a
stroll around the room, thought he saw on a small
table in a corner a vessel containing water: so
whether he instantly became very thirsty, or wished

 to wash the ale off his
face, he climbed upon the
table, and approaching the
vessel thrust his head into
it — but he lost his balance
and tumbled half way in.

It was Huggermugger's inkstand — and the dwarf had
some difficulty in getting out. When he did so, his
head and one half his body was ink-black, while the
other was its original color. He did not dare to show
himself to his friends in this plight, so he slunk into
a dark corner till the feast should break up.

Another half-tipsy deserter of the jovial company, happening to see a rat-trap open, and still baited with cheese (the rats themselves seemed to have all dis-appeared since the giant's de-parture) walked straight into it — when down went the iron gratings, and he was caught. Becoming alarmed, he called to his com-panions — but it was some time  before anybody came ; when they did, they danced around the cage, laughing at him, and poking him with sticks, and it was some time before the poor fellow was let out.

Meanwhile the sun went down, the twilight stole on, and still they kept up the revel. The moon rose and shone in through the great window, and they had no need of candles. As the night advanced, how-ever, the sky became overcast. Distant thunder was heard. Wild masses of dark cloud drifted across the moon, which now shone bright, now was buried in the clouds. The revelry was at its wildest, when a nearer peal of thunder startled and sobered some of the more timorous. Something nearer and darker than a cloud seemed to overshadow them — and looking up at the great window, what should they see, or fancy they saw, but the great faces of the Huggermuggers between them and the moon, gazing sorrowfully down upon them. The panic spread at once. Rushing, scrambling, tumbling over each other, pitching almost head-foremost down from the table, away they scampered as fast as they could in their tipsy condition. Fast as they could they made for the door, and fled in the desperation of fear, rolling and tumbling down the stairs — and not one was left behind, save Kobboltozo and his friend Hammawhaxo, the carpenter. They alone were sober, cool, and collected. Besides, they had a motive for remaining, and were not sorry that they were left alone in the hall of the Huggermuggers.

STAMPEDE OF THE DWARFS.

CHAPTER SIX.

THE SEARCH OF KOBBOLTOZO AND HAMMAWHAXO.

HE great room was no sooner cleared of the frightened dwarfs, than Kobboltozo and Hammawhaxo each lit a candle, and approached the secret closet in which the ancient Hugger manuscript had been discovered. What their object was I will tell you.

When Hammawhaxo first saw this old manuscript, (the Huggermuggers were living in their house then, you may remember,) he had no time to peruse it thoroughly, but only got a hasty look into it, for he was afraid of being detected by the giant and his wife. But he read enough to learn the fatal secret, the divulging of which is supposed to have been the

cause of the misfortunes which befell them. He read,
you remember, that the Huggermugger race had
become great by eating of a particular kind of shell-
fish, while the dwarfs stopped growing at a certain
period, and began to grow crooked. Also, that if this
secret were told to more than one person out of the
Huggermugger family, some great calamity would
befall the last survivor of the race. This secret the
carpenter, (who perhaps did not bear any positive
malice towards the giant,) in a heedless hour, imparted
to the shoemaker.

But it was not enough for Kobboltozo that he had
ruined the giant's happiness. He imagined that it was
a possible thing to become a giant himself. He could
not bear to live and die a dwarf. He would have
given all that he owned, and all the little heart and
soul that he had, to boot, to be able to stand in
Huggermugger's shoes, to put on Huggermugger's
boots and stride as he did across the country. To be
Huggermugger's equal — to be able to thunder in a
voice like his, and sit in his great arm-chair—to make
the other dwarfs bow down like slaves before him —
to rule in the island by fear, and not as the good
giant did, by justice and kindness, was his constant

ambition and dream. Now, since the giant was gone, it became his darling *hope*.

"That manuscript," he said to himself, "at which the carpenter got but a glimpse, must contain more secrets worth knowing. Where is this mysterious shell-fish — what is it? Why should not I profit by it? And how long would it take to grow out of my dwarfish limits into strong exulting gianthood?" Such thoughts burned in the cobbler's heart day and night, and gave him no rest. He did not see that true greatness is far from consisting in size or the possession of power.

"And now, at last," he thought, "my way is clear. I shall obtain the old manuscript and shall know all. If my fate condemns me to be no bigger, no handsomer than I am, I must submit: but if this manuscript holds out any hope, be sure I shall not be slow in availing myself of it."

So Kobboltozo was not sorry that his companions had been frightened away, for the night and solitude were favorable to his schemes. He would have preferred, perhaps, to be entirely alone, and that none should know the full contents of the manuscript but himself. But he could do nothing without Hamma-

whaxo: first in finding the sliding panel in the wall,
and secondly in helping him to decipher the ancient
Hugger writing. So it was previously agreed that
the carpenter should remain.

With eager steps they hastened to the door of the
secret closet, and with trembling hands pushed back
the sliding panel. But to their great surprise and
vexation they found nothing there. For it will be
remembered that the giant had taken it out before his
departure, and sunk it in a deep well under the rocks.
At first Kobboltozo was disposed to think that his
friend had deceived him with a false story, but this
idea soon passed, and on reflection he concluded that
the giant had concealed it somewhere else. He was
almost certain that Huggermugger had not taken it
with him, for he had seen him carry scarcely any thing
to the ship.

Swallowing down his disappointment then as well
as he could, he proposed to Hammawhaxo that they
should commence searching the whole house. Hammawhaxo, though not so solicitous about the matter as
his friend, consented to help him. So they went first
round and round the room, tapping on the walls,
poking into all the closets, and cracks, and corners.

Then they went into all the other rooms, peeping into drawers, and boxes, and chests—turning things upside down and inside out—ransacking from garret to cellar. Sometimes they would light on some old scrap of parchment, yellow with age, and from which the writing was almost faded. But they could make out nothing. As near as could be guessed, they were only fragments of old love-letters that had passed between the giant and his wife—how many years ago, who knows?

In fine, the dwarfs looked everywhere except down the well, where the Hugger manuscript was soaking; and which, if they could ever have succeeded in fishing up, would have been so faded and blurred, that they could never have read a line of it.

Meanwhile, the thunder, which had rolled heavily in the distance, came nearer and nearer. Through the great windows the lightning blazed, almost extinguishing the light of their feeble candles. The carpenter became uneasy, and proposed that they should abandon their search for that night, as it was evident a storm was fast coming on.

"We had better go," said he, "we can come again to-morrow. It is more comfortable at home than in this dreary great castle. The rain will be pouring down soon. Hark! how the wind roars in the trees and on the roof. Come!"

"Presently," said Kobboltozo. "There is one place we have not yet thoroughly explored. I thought I noticed a little door at one end of the cellar. It may be that the manuscript is hid there. Let us take one look: we shan't be but a moment. It would be a pity not to look. To-morrow we may not have so good a chance: for the dwarfs will be again here, lounging about. and we must conceal our purposes from them."

So. much to the carpenter's reluctance, they descended the steps to the cellar, each with a blazing torch in his hand. They went along till they came to a corner, where Kobboltozo fancied he had seen the little door. And, sure enough, there was a door, just large enough for them to creep through. They easily drew back the bolt, and after a few stout tugs, the door, which from the cobwebs about it appeared to have been long closed, opened, and they peeped in. It seemed to be a low vaulted cell of some length. They entered, and crept cautiously along. The floor soon began to slope downwards; but they still groped along till they came to steps. Descending these, they were stopped by another door, much larger than the first. They deliberated some time whether they should open it. Hammawhaxo was for returning: Kobboltozo for going on.

"Just this door," he said; "we will just peep in, and if we don't find what we want, we will return." So he slid back the bolt of this door also, and with a push it yielded. They entered, and found themselves in a very large cave, hewn out of the solid rock. There seemed to be nothing in it—but on the walls, as well as they could see by the light of their flickering torches, were inscriptions in huge letters, of the ancient Hugger language, cut in the walls. These excited their curiosity. "Perhaps," said Kobboltozo, "these inscriptions will tell us something about the mys-

terious shell-fish." So they went round and round, trying to decipher them. But the letters were so large, and reached up so high in the darkness, and

their torches threw so dim a light. that they could not
make out a single word.

" Come," said Kobboltozo, at last, " let's go now ;
we shall discover nothing to-night. We can return
to this place to-morrow and continue our search.
Why, really, the storm is coming. I can hear the
wind and the thunder even through these thick walls."

They turned to retrace their steps, but a sudden
gust of wind from some door or crevice blew violently
against them. and in an instant both their torches were
extinguished.

CHAPTER SEVEN.

GROPINGS UNDER GROUND.

HE two dwarfs groped round and round the great cave, but could not find the door by which they entered. "What the deuce shall we do?" they said; "this is a most unfortunate business!" "Why didn't you look well where the door was?" said one. "Why didn't you return before the wind arose!" said the other. "Why did you stop to look at those letters on the wall?" said the carpenter; "you knew you couldn't read them!" "Why didn't you bring along some matches to relight our torches?" said the cobbler. "And why didn't you bring a covered lantern?" said the carpenter. "If you had only had your wits about you," said the cobbler, "you would have taken a better look into that manuscript, and ascertained where the wonderful shell-fish were to be found, and then we needn't have got ourselves into this hole!"

" Confound your old manuscript, with the shell-fish," said the carpenter. " I wish to heavens I had never seen it, or told you any thing about it, and then I should have been safe and snug in my bed at home!"

And so grumbling at each other, they groped about in the impenetrable darkness ; and instead of helping and sympathizing with each other, selfish beings that they were, they did nothing but lay the cause of their misfortune on each other's shoulders.

At last they found in the darkness an opening, which they supposed was the door. But they were mistaken. It was only another passage, leading them still further underneath the ground. There was nothing to do now but wait till morning, or go on groping their way in the darkness, hoping by and by to reach an opening in the rocks by which they might extricate themselves from this gloomy and dangerous place. Gloomy it certainly was. and, for aught they knew, dangerous, for they were fearful every moment of plunging headlong into some deep hole or well.

After awhile, finding no outlet, and fearing to go on, they concluded to sit or lie down, and wait patiently for the morning light — if indeed the morning light ever came into that dark labyrinth. So they sat down and waited, with their backs against the damp sides of the cavern. The night seemed endlessly long. At last they thought they perceived a faint, dim light, so they continued their way. Sometimes the passage grew wide and high ; sometimes it was so low and narrow that they could hardly squeeze through. At length it grew gradually wider and higher, and descended rapidly. Soon it began to grow less dark, and they could see the roofs of the winding galleries through which they passed hung with stalactites and crystals. It continued to grow lighter, but with a tinge as of a distant fire-light, not the clear white sunshine. What could this be ? was it a subterranean fire they were approaching ?

Larger and more splendid became the hanging stalactites and crystals. Great blocks of marble — white, green, and red — of porphyry, jasper, malachite. agate, carnelian, lapis lazuli, lay heaped in confusion around. And now the walls and ceilings were all powdered and frosted over with marble and silver—now glowed

with crystallizations of copper, platina, or zinc :—and
now it was all gold—gold growing and branching out
into every sort of fantastic design—gold blossoming
like fern or coral, or clinging to the stone like
sponges or fungi—gold streaking and veining the
rocks. And now, behold, all manner of precious
stones, that seemed to blossom like flowers amid the
gold and silver leaf-work—flowers of diamond, ruby,
carbuncle, emerald, topaz, garnet, sapphire—all glowing more intensely, as the two dwarfs advanced, in
the mysterious fire-light which they were approaching.

There seemed to be no end to these gorgeous chambers and galleries. Sometimes, tempted by the splen-
dor of these gold plants and gems, they endeavored
to tear or break off a branch of the metal leaves, or
a bunch of diamonds or rubies. It resisted all their
efforts, and they were forced to leave it. They were
lost in wonder at all this strange and unheard of
magnificence. " Have we then reached the centre of
the earth." they thought, "and are these the secret
laboratories and treasure-houses of the earth?"

At last they approached a great door, gorgeous to
behold, before which hung what appeared to be a
great curtain of pure gold-leaf and amber, inwrought

with thousands of diamonds, and sapphires, and rubies. This curtain seemed to be semi-transparent, and it was behind this and through this that the great red light was glowing, which they had seen so far off among the caves.

The dwarfs raised one corner of this curtain and entered. They were struck dumb with wonder and amazement at what they saw.

CHAPTER EIGHT.

THE GNOMES.

T was the dwelling and laboratory of those elfs who work under ground — called Gnomes.

The dwarfs found themselves in a vast hall or dome, in the centre of which seemed to be a huge furnace, from which issued great flames. But what was very strange, they could feel no heat, they could hear no crackling, they could see no smoke. The flames were like those of the Northern-lights, only redder and intenser—indeed, so intense that the dwarfs who had been so long in the darkness, could hardly bear to look at them. On drawing nearer, they were astonished to see against the light, swarms of little beings of strange and grotesque shapes, and all of one sober brown or grey color, like the rocks around,

So they proceeded in the way so vaguely indicated
by the gnomes, and soon found themselves in a gal-
lery which led them through several such caverns as
those they had already traversed. Gradually the red
fire-light which issued from the hall of the gnomes
grew fainter and fainter, till they found themselves at
last in utter darkness. Soon, however, a faint light,
as from without, seemed to dawn, dimly revealing the
rough sides of the cavern. Encouraged, they pushed
on through the narrow windings—now up, now down
—now interrupted in their journey by huge masses of
fallen rock, now by streams of water—till to their
great joy they at last reached an opening in the side
of a rocky gorge, from which they saw the sunlight
again, and the blue sea sleeping beneath them.

CHAPTER NINE.

THE WITCH'S CAVE.

 HIS opening, in which they emerged, proved to be a small cave, which had the appearance of having once been inhabited. The walls and ceiling were a good deal smoked. There was an opening which had evidently served as a chimney, and a piece of an old rusty lamp which had been fastened to the wall still remained. But whoever had lived there, it must have been centuries since, they thought, for not only weeds, and grass, and flowers, but moss and lichens were growing abundantly on the rocks and between the stones. In one corner they thought they saw something resembling remains of human bones, half buried beneath the earth. But what inter-

THE WITCH'S CAVE.

ested Kobboltozo was to discover on one side of the
cave a rude, half-effaced inscription, in letters not un-
like those in the great cavern where they had lost
their way. What could this place be? What was
the mysterious connection between this cave, and the
region of the gnomes, and the dwelling of the giants?
Suddenly a thought flashed across Kobboltozo's brain,
and he ran to the opening of the cave, and looked out
to discover on what part of the island they were. The
cave opened upon a narrow and steep ravine, down
which there were rude steps, not easy to ascend or
descend, leading from the cave's mouth to the bottom
of the rocks, whence a path conducted to the sea-
shore.

Kobboltozo having made this discovery, came running back to his companion in a state of great excitement.

"It is—it is the very place!" he cried. "A lucky
star has guided us to this spot! Know then, my
friend, that this is the Witch's Cave—that very witch
who came with the ancestor's of the Huggermuggers
to this island, and who foretold to them the growth
and prosperity of their race."

For you must know that there was a tradition

among the dwarfs that such a witch had formerly
lived somewhere in this very gorge. But no one had
ever ventured up the difficult steps, or had discovered
the place of her abode. A sort of superstitious fear,
too, had effectually deterred them from entering this
wild and gloomy ravine.

"We have found it — we have found it!" cried
Kobboltozo; "there's no doubt of this being the place.
Ever since you told me of your glimpse at the secret
of the giant race, I have thought of this ancient witch,
and the tradition of this ravine. And to think that our
bad luck in getting lost leads us to this spot, and
turns out to be good luck after all. Aha! I begin to
see! Was it then by this long dark labyrinth through
which we have passed, that the witch held communi-
cation with those gnomes — those queer goblins of the
earth? And was it these gnomes who helped the
Huggermuggers to build their house?"—

"And these letters on the wall — what are they?
Come, Hamm, you are a bit of a scholar. Help me
to spell out what remains of the inscription."

"Willingly," said the other. "but I fear, Kobb. that
we can't get much satisfactory information from these
half effaced characters."

" We'll try, at any rate," said the shoemaker.

So they set their wits together, but found themselves much puzzled to spell out any thing clearly. All they could make of it was something like this translation : —

. . . . CAVE OF THE SEA . . . . .

UND . . ROCKS . . . . RIGHT HAND . . .

. . . . . . SHELL FI . . . . . MER-KING . . . . . .

. . . . WAVES . . . STILL . . . . . GIANT . . . .

" Well, but this is something, at any rate," said Kobboltozo. " It gives some clue to what we are seeking. It seems we must find a Cave of the Sea, lying somewhere under the rocks, to the right hand, after we have descended the ravine ; that there we may find the shell-fish. But what is this about the mer-king, and the waves? Must we call up the mer-king, and ask him where the wonderful shell-fish are? Yes, that must be it — and it must be done when the waves are perfectly still. We'll do it."

" But," said the carpenter, " we must have an incantation."

" What's that ? " said the shoemaker.

" Why, some sort of spell, or rhyme, and something scattered on the waves, while we repeat a verse
or so, or some old words of the Hugger language.
I hardly know — but I've heard that that's the way
the witches do. Let's try it. You compliment me on
being a bit of a scholar — do you know I'm a bit of
a poet too, and often sing my rhymes to myself while
I am hammering or planing?"

" Very well ; now set your wits agoing, and make
some verses for the occasion — a sort of what do you
call it — incantation? "

So, half in fun, half in earnest, Hammawhaxo ham-
mered out some lines — and repeated them over to
himself till he had got them by heart.

After satisfying themselves that there was nothing
else in the witch's cave that could afford them any
help in their search, they began the difficult descent
of the steep rocks. It was not an easy matter to get
down, and several times they came near breaking their
necks. But at last they reached the bottom of the
gorge. A path, or rather the dry bed of a stream
led them down to the seashore, where, having allayed
their hunger somewhat with some berries they found,
they stretched themselves out on the grass under the

rocks. There, what with their fatigue and excitement, the cool, soft turf on which they lay, and the soothing murmur of the sea lapping on the beach, they both fell into a profound sleep.

CHAPTER TEN.

KOBBOLTOZO'S DREAM.

OBBOLTOZO fell asleep with his brain full of witches, mermen, shell-fish, giants, and gnomes. So it was very natural he should dream. And he did dream a wonderful dream, as he afterwards told the carpenter, and which the carpenter (said the tailor) told me. Kobboltozo dreamed that he was walking in the palace of the king of the gnomes. His majesty was bigger than the other gnomes, his subjects, and not at all silent like them; on the contrary, he was very talkative and merry. Kobboltozo asked him, of course, the question which was always uppermost in his mind — where he should find the wonderful shell-fish of the giants.

"That's a secret," said the king, "which no one here knows but myself. It is well you asked me. Come with me."

So they passed through room after room, more splendid than any thing he had yet seen — all was gold, silver, and precious stones — and knocked at a door, which opened, and disclosed a long avenue leading to the sea.

"Take this path," said the king, "and it will conduct you to what you desire — but first fill your pockets with as much gold and as many precious stones as you want." Kobboltozo did so, and bidding the king adieu, the door closed behind him.

Immediately he seemed to have wings to his feet, for he flew in an instant to the sea. When he reached the shore, he found it covered with a strange kind of shell-fish he had never seen. He took one of these, and it opened its shell of itself, as if asking to be eaten. It had a singular but not an unpleasant flavor. So he ate another and another. Presently he began to grow, and grow, and grow. He seemed to be inflating like a balloon, till he found himself larger than Huggermugger, and a good deal handsomer. With huge strides he walked across the island, his pockets full of the gold and jewels the gnome had given him. He reached the village of the dwarfs — and saw his own little workshop, and all the other houses, and all the dwarfs running about pursuing their business, and felt the most supreme contempt for them all, and the most unbounded admiration of himself. It delighted him to see how they ran away from him, or fell on their knees before him, or did whatever he bid them do. "Poor little beings," he said, "I shan't make shoes for you any longer — a greater than Huggermugger is among you — you shall all be my slaves — I will do with you whatever I please — am I not the greatest of the giants?"

'(I don't mean to say, said the tailor. that Kobboltozo told all this to Hammawhaxo — it is only what we dwarfs thought he said in his dream.)

Having thrown a few gold pieces to the dwarfs, he strode to the giant's house, and was immensely delighted to find how the great mansion fitted him. Only he would have had it bigger still.

No sooner had he expressed this wish, than the king of the gnomes again stood before him.

"Ah," thought Kobboltozo, "he has come up through those subterranean passages I discovered. He

also shall do my bidding." So he told the king to
bring him a thousand gnomes, and pull down Huggermugger's house, and build one twice as large. The
gnome king nodded, and disappeared. Presently he
appeared again, followed by an immense swarm of
little brown elfs, who set to work and pulled down
the house. Pretty soon they built one twice as large.
"Now," said Kobboltozo, "cover it all over with gold
and diamonds and rubies." And they brought up gold
and diamonds and rubies, and covered the house all
over with them. But as they were finishing, they
heard thunder, and the witch of the ravine appeared
in the midst of the gnomes, with a countenance full
of anger, and stamped her foot — when suddenly the
gnomes all disappeared and left him alone with the
witch.

Kobboltozo rose up to
annihilate the old woman
with one blow of his
mighty arm, when it was
suddenly seized by some-
thing sharp, which held
him fast. Turning around,

he found his arm actually caught in the thorns of a

great blackberry bush, which in his sleep he had rolled against — and there was an end to his magnificent dream.

CHAPTER ELEVEN.

THE MER-KING.

OBBOLTOZO sat up and rubbed his eyes, and looked with intense hatred and disgust at the innocent black-berry bush, which had scratched to pieces his splendid dream. Seeing Hammawhaxo still asleep, he expended upon him a part of his ill-nature in waking him without ceremony. "Come, comrade," he cried, shaking him, "it is time we were going. We have a great deal to do. We must call up the mer-king while the waves are still, and yonder are the rocks where I have no doubt we shall see his cave. Come, get your — what do you call it — incantation all ready. Get up, man — don't be going to sleep again!"

So poor Hammawhaxo was roused up, and followed his companion slowly along the beach towards the

5

rocks. There they were not long in discovering a
cave, having a narrow opening on one side to the
sea, and an equally narrow entrance from the land.
They entered. It was very large and dark, the only
light being that which came through the above mentioned opening to the sea. Nearly the whole of the
grotto was filled with the water, which appeared to
be of immense depth, and of an exquisite emerald
green hue. The sea was so quiet that the wavelets
hardly whispered against the sides of the dark cavern.
It was a weird and solemn place. There was a narrow ledge on which they could walk, and here the
two dwarfs took their stand.

"Are you ready with your speech?" said Kobboltozo. "All ready," said his companion. They then
threw into the water some shells and bunches of sea-
weed; and repeated these lines: —

> King of the mysterious sea,
> Tell us where the power may be,
> Which may set our bodies free
> From the enchanter's tyranny.
> Where the wondrous food may be
> Which will make us great as he
> Who was giant here, while we
> Are but dwarfs of low degree!

They looked into the deep, clear, emerald water, and waited in silence. At last there was a heaving and a bubbling up from below, and soon a vast, dim, colorless shape, half appearing, half hidden in the green water, waved to and fro beneath them. Then there rose a gigantic head,* crowned with magnificent pearls, and coral, and amber, and sea-flowers—an apparition with flowing locks and beard that seemed to mingle with the white foam—and great calm blue eyes that gazed solemnly upon them—and a low voice, in a surfy cadence, chanted this reply:—

> Not in the Ocean deep and clear,
> Not on the Land so broad and fair,
> Not in the regions of boundless Air,
> Not in the Fire's burning sphere—-
> 'Tis not here—'tis not there.
> Ye may seek it everywhere.
> He that is a dwarf in spirit
> Never shall the isle inherit.
> Hearts that grow 'mid daily cares
> Grow to greatness unawares;
> Noble souls alone may know
> How the giants live and grow.

The water heaved once more in long swells—breaking and sparkling and eddying in the unearthly light

* See Frontispiece.

of the grotto — as the dim shape disappeared and sunk in the sea.

There was something in the solemnity of the place, and the strange vision, which seemed to impress the words of this reply deeply upon the memory of these two men. But it was more the words than the sense, for it had a meaning they did not altogether comprehend. They turned and left the cave. For some time neither of them spoke a word. They were both sunk in their own thoughts. The appearance of the mer-king had somewhat astonished and awed them ; for it was half in jest and unbelief that they had summoned him. The answer disappointed and puzzled them.

"If the wonderful shell-fish," said Kobboltozo, " is not to be found in the sea, nor on the earth, nor in the air. nor in the fire — where the deuce *is* it to be found ? "

" Why don't you see ? " said Hammawhaxo, "if it isn't to be found *in* the sea, it may be found *on* the sea : if it isn't to be found *on* the ground, it must be *in* or *under* the ground."

" Good ! capital ! " cried the shoemaker. " Why, Hamm. you have a shrewd wit. I should never have

thought of that now. That must be it, without doubt.
I'll tell you what, now. We'll divide our labors, and
when we've found our treasure we'll divide the profits.
You shall pursue your search *on* the sea, and I mine
under the ground. It's a bargain, isn't it?"

"Well," said the carpenter, "we can try. I must
confess I should like the fun of sailing about a little.
I always had a sort of hankering after a sea life, and
sometimes almost wish I had gone off with those
American sailors who were here — though I should
have felt rather uneasy, with Huggermugger for a
fellow passenger. And as for *you*, old Kobb, you
certainly have a fancy for making discoveries under
ground. So we'll think about your plan. Let's go
home now; we are many miles away from the village,
and we must get back before nightfall."

CHAPTER TWELVE.

THE EFFECTS OF TELLING SECRETS.

 ow Hammawhaxo had a wife, and it is very natural for wives to desire to know what has happened, when their husbands are out all night and a great part of next day. Some wives *will* know their husbands' secrets, and *may* not keep them safely locked after they have them.

Mrs. Hammawhaxo (to tell the truth) loved to visit and gossip.

In fine, the best intentioned wives, if they are endowed with a social disposition, will sometimes let a secret escape — not all at once, but little by little, like a leaky bucket.

And so it happened — that which was whispered in the ear was soon buzzed about, and then trumpeted from one house to another, till the whole community of dwarfs knew something of the giant's secret, and of the events we have been narrating.

It was whispered that Kobboltozo and Hammawhaxo had entered into partnership in the oyster and other shell-fish business. And now the whole village was in a state of excitement, and every one was preparing to commence the shell-fish business on his own account. "Is it possible," they said. "that we have been all our lives living here, within reach of this wonderful shell-fish, and have never found it? What wouldn't we give to grow to be giants! We would give all that we have—houses, gardens, trades, wives, children, peace, and happiness — all — to find this wondrous food."

My friends (said Stitchkin) I needn't tell you all the details of this unfortunate business. Look there, at those houses and fences tumbling to pieces — those gardens overgrown with weeds — this whole village deserted and dead. They will tell you more forcibly than I can, the sad fate that befell us.

And yet hardly any of them bore *me* any good will.

They laughed at me, or were cold towards me, because I didn't join them or sympathize with them in
their mad and ruinous enterprises. And when I did
all I could to dissuade them from giving themselves
up to a vain and fruitless search, after what I knew
they never could find, they treated me as an enemy,
and I had no peace or enjoyment as long as they
were near me.

As soon as the fatal secret was known, our people
began to desert their homes and daily occupations and
encamped in numbers near the sea-shore, where they
spent days and nights in looking for new species of
shell-fish. But they rarely found any. When they
did, there was no end to their selfish and envious
quarrels. They would wade into the sea, and dig in
the sand, and suffer wet and fatigue and hunger all
day; and if two or three happened to light at the
same time upon any strange bivalve, they would stand
and dispute about it all day. Sometimes they organ-
ized little companies, and when they had collected a
number of shells, some one would steal them and
hide them. These companies never held together long.
Then each man would seek for himself, and so increase the labor by not having it shared.

THE SCRABBLE FOR SHELL-FISH.

Sometimes one fellow would find an enormous clam or oyster, and stand sentinel over it all day, or begin devouring it; or he would deliberately sit down upon it, defending his property, tooth and nail, against all unlawful claimants, and, when night came, carry it off to some secret place.

Did you ever notice a parcel of chickens, when one has found a worm or a bit of mouldy bread? No. 1, the finder, picks up worm and runs, followed hard by No. 2. No. 3 and 4 join in the pursuit, and twenty more. No. 1 drops his worm, which is seized by No. 25. No. 25 is dodged and run down, and relinquishes worm to No. 40, who in turn is persecuted by 45, 46, and 47. Finally, No. 50, being the longest legged and greediest, succeeds in getting ahead of the runners, and bolts down the worm. And so the farce ends, to commence over again the next time a worm turns up.

Just such a farce went on every day among the dwarfs, except that sometimes it turned into a tragedy. Bloody battles sometimes took place among them. Sometimes the waves would wash them away and drown them. Some fell sick, or died from exposure to the hot sun or the damp night air, or from having

gormandized upon the shell-fish. Some of them took
a fancy, as Kobboltozo did, that the giants' food was
to be found in caves, or by burrowing in the earth.
Many of them went under ground, and never returned. In fine, all was disorder, strife, and disunion.
And, in the mean time, their houses, and shops, and
gardens were totally neglected — until all became as
you see.

As for myself (said Stitchkin) I remained at home
as long as I could; but no one brought me any work,
and I became poor. But for all that, I couldn't bear
to see my fellow-beings suffer, even through their own
folly; and I spent many a night nursing the sick,
many a day trying to settle some foolish quarrel, or
endeavoring to persuade my neighbors to return to
their occupations. I tried to show them that we small
people were evidently intended by Providence to be
as we are — that mere size did not constitute happiness — that we could not change our natures — that as
long as we followed the path allotted to us, we should
be happy and prosperous, but while we spent our lives
in seeking for the impossible, we should be miserable.
Some listened to my advice — when it was too late.
Sickness and death had already seized upon them.

"But what became of Hammawhaxo and Kobbol-tozo?" said Mr. Nabbum.

Neither of them became giants, I believe, (said the tailor.) Hammawhaxo had a boat, which he made for himself. He rigged it up with a mast and sail, and, one moonlight night, he and his wife, and a few friends sailed off on a voyage of discovery. His little vessel was seen for some days cruising about, as if seeking for something, then sailed to the north. One day there came on a storm, and he never returned.

As for Kobboltozo, it is not clearly known yet what became of him either. He was seen last entering a cave, which is supposed to lead to vast subterranean chambers. It is said that some others followed him, and found him seated beside a pile of enormous oysters, which he was busily devouring, and that he seemed to be in an unnatural state of jovial excitement, and expressed no intention of returning. Those who saw him left him there, and returned; so that the probability is that he is still under ground, or that he has lost his way and perished.

I have now (said Stitchkin) told you all I know about the fate of our race. In the main, we have brought about our own destruction. But there were

some of us who perhaps deserved a better fate—some
who regretted the misfortunes of the giants, and looked
upon them more as benefactors than as enemies—
who, had it not been for the malice and the selfish
ambition of Kobboltozo, would still have made good
and useful members of our little community.

As for Hammawhaxo, I always thought he had a
great deal that was good in him. It was an unfortunate curiosity which made him the first to become
acquainted with the giants' secret: and a pardonable
want of thought — say even a confiding and unsuspicious nature — which induced him to whisper it in
the shoemaker's ear. I can't think he entertained any
positive ill will towards Huggermugger. But he erred
sadly in having any thing to do with Kobboltozo, after
he saw the unhappy results of having imparted to him
the secret. He erred in not taking a decided and bold
stand against him, rather than siding with him and
entering tamely into his schemes.

CHAPTER THIRTEEN.

ACKY CABLE and Mr. Nabbum thought the tailor's narrative very strange and wonderful : and the latter proposed that they should remain in the island till they had ascertained all the facts about the disappearance and destruction of the dwarfs. "The fact is, Jacky," said Zebedee, "they *wer'nt* dwarfs, except along side of them giants, but were every bit as big as we, and maybe a leetle bigger — and I guess in Ameriky they'd almost take the shine off the Kentucky giant. So you see, I feel a kind o' feller feeling for them, and I for one should like to undertake an exploring expedition in search of some of 'em."

As for Stitchkin, they proposed that he should leave his lonely little house, and come with them on board ship, which the little tailor gladly assented to. So the three left the ruined village and returned to the ship together. The sailors heard the whole story of the dwarfs, and Stitchkin became soon a great favorite among them. Every day some of them would make excursions on shore, under his guidance, where they found enough to do in seeing the wonders of the island.

One day Nabbum, Jacky, and Stitchkin, were on shore collecting some of the great shells and other interesting products of the island, when they saw a queer little sailing vessel coming round a projecting point of the rocks, and holding directly towards them. They were much excited, of course, by this apparition, for they supposed they were alone in the island, and couldn't imagine where the little vessel could come from.

"Well now," said Nabbum, "if this aint curous! I want to know! That's about the rummest little craft that ever *I* see. Who do you 'spose is aboard of her ?"

"I can't imagine," said Jacky. "I'm prepared now

for any thing, after the astonishing stories we've heard. It would take a good deal to surprise me now. If you told me there was a crew of gnomes aboard, with an amber sail, and a gold rudder and keel, bringing in a load of carbuncles — or if you should say it was the old witch of the ravine come to life, I should about believe you. What do you say, Mr. Stitchkin?"

The tailor stood gazing in dumb bewilderment — when suddenly he clapped his hands and shouted with surprise and delight —

" Why, if it isn't — no, it can't be — yes, it must be — it is — it is Hammawhaxo, or else his ghost ! Don't you see him — don't you remember him?"

"No !" cried Nabbum, " do tell — you don't say so — I-I-I sw—an !"

" Let's hail him," they cried, "perhaps he don't see us. Sloop ahoy !" and an answering shout was sent back from the vessel. They ran to the edge of the beach, and very soon the little vessel put directly in for the shore, and Hammawhaxo jumped out; and he and the tailor, who probably had scarcely ever even shaken hands before, rushed into each other's arms.

When the first greetings were over, the carpenter made hasty inquiries about the other dwarfs. When

he heard the sad news that they had all either died
or been lost, his countenance became much troubled,
and the tears stood in his eyes. "Ah," he said, "it
is my fault, my miserable weakness. Why did I
ever betray the good giant — how could I ever league
myself with that cursed — no, I won't curse him —
he is punished enough, poor fellow! And I, my
friends — will you believe it? — I am a changed man.
Suffering, grief, remorse I have had. I am not what
I was. But let me tell you my story. .

"But, first of all, forgive me, my good Stitchkin,
if I have ever said or done any thing to injure you."

"You never have," said the tailor, much affected.

"I don't know," said the carpenter, "I may have
done so — I was a miserable, weak, selfish wretch. I
am changed. I hope to live to do some good yet."

Hammawhaxo then told them how he had sailed
away in search of the wonderful shell-fish, according
to agreement with Kobboltozo. But it was partly, he
said, because he liked the pleasure of sailing — for he
did not much believe in Kobboltozo's fancies. He told
how he went to sea with a fair wind, and sailed a
good many leagues to the north — how a storm came
up and upset his vessel, how his wife and his com-

panions were drowned, and how he escaped by swimming, and reached an island, which he found inhabited by a race of civilized and cultivated people — how he lived among them — how he had thought over his past life, and had determined to be a better and a more useful man — how, at last, he began to long to return to his own island, and to do some good among his people. "So I bought me yonder little sloop," he said, "and bidding these good people adieu, sailed for our island. God grant that I am not too late, for I cannot but think we shall find again some of our missing companions."

CHAPTER FOURTEEN.

THE FATE OF KOBBOLTOZO.

ND now you must hear the strangest part of my narrative," said the carpenter. " It relates to Kobboltozo. As I drew near our island, the wind took me to a part of it where I had never been, and I was obliged to moor my little bark under some steep rocks. There I found one of those caves, of which our island seems to be so full, and far in its deepest recesses I saw—what remains of Kobboltozo."

" Is he dead, then?" they asked.

" No—on the contrary he is living in a state of the most perfect contentment with himself and every thing else. He has found at last, he thinks, the giant's shell-fish. And a wonderful shell-fish indeed it must be — though its effects are rather different from what might be expected. Kobboltozo lives in that dim cave, and does nothing but eat oysters and smile at his reflection in the water, and strut up and down like a peacock — for he imagines that he is growing larger and handsomer every day. But the wonderful part of it is that, really, instead of getting hold of the genuine article, he feeds on something possessing just the opposite quality. He is in reality growing rapidly smaller and more disproportioned, instead of larger and shapelier. His head remains its original size, while his legs seem to be dwindling to mere spider's legs!

"And what do you think he was doing when I first discovered him? He was standing on a huge pyramid of empty oyster shells, in the attitude of some mighty sultan, with the whole world beneath him as his obedient slave, and soliloquizing in this way: — 'Having risen to these magnifi-  cent heights of power, I shall grow to still greater. This island shall be subject to our will. But this island shall be no more than our footstool: our power

shall extend to other lands — a world of serfs shall do
us reverence.   We shall'——

"Here," said Hammawhaxo, "his majesty, the cobbler, discovered me, and recognized his old comrade.
'Hah!' he cried, 'this low-born slave, this son of the
hammer and saw! we knew him once, methinks — he
shall be our grand vizier, our minister of state, for the
fellow has been serviceable to me.   Approach, carpenter, and receive the honor we intend for thee!'

"'Come, old Kobb.' said I, 'leave these ridiculous
airs — you are no more a king than I am.   Come
down from that pile of oyster shells, and take your
hat and come with me.   Leave this dark cavern, where
you have no companions but bats, water-rats, and sea-
birds, and let's go back to our village.'

"'*Your* village. not mine,' said Kobboltozo, 'no miserable dwarfs for me — let them perish — let them
waste away with fevers — let them kill one another —
let them lose themselves in caves and holes of the
earth.   What care I!   We will invoke the gnomes or
the mermen, and they will bring us a ship — we will
invade other countries. and bring back their nobles
and their fair women captives, and found a new gov-
ernment here'——

"He was going on in this strain, when I again interrupted him, by proposing that he should come with me; that I had a vessel all ready.

"He shook his head and smiled, and looked at me with majestic contempt. 'Some day,' he said, 'we shall come, and you will recognize us as your giant king — for the present, it pleases our sovereign will to remain here!'

"Finding it useless to reason with him, I was obliged to abandon him to his fate.

"So there the infatuated fellow remains, eating his oysters, and dwindling away to a mere insect. In a year from this time, I calculate that he will be just about the size of a pin's head."

THE SHOEMAKER'S LAST.

CHAPTER FIFTEEN.

A BEGINNING AND AN ENDING.

 TITCHKIN was mistaken in imagining that so many of the dwarfs had been lost or had perished. There was quite a number of them, both men and women, who had lost their way, while seeking after the giant's shell-fish, and had come out in another part of the island. They proved to be more rational than many of the others, and kept together. forming a little association, which got along tolerably well. They found a quite beautiful and fertile spot near the southern shore, which they had cultivated: and they succeeded so well that they gradually abandoned the idea of becoming giants, and built up a little settlement. where they

devoted themselves to farming, fishing, and the trades
to which they had been accustomed. They found this
spot better situated, being nearer the sea than the village they had abandoned, which was some way inland,
and the soil of which was full of rocks and stones.

This little settlement was discovered one day by
Hammawhaxo and Stitchkin, as they were sailing in
the carpenter's little vessel round the island. The
dwarfs were delighted to see their old acquaintances,
and the carpenter and tailor no less so to find so
many of their tribe left alive and flourishing.

So they determined to come and settle down there
too. The tailor's kindness to those who had suffered,
had softened many hearts towards him; and Hammawhaxo, who during his absence had acquired a good
deal of useful knowledge, made himself very serviceable to the little community. First, he drew a map
of the island, then he discovered a path (made formerly by the giants) leading from the new settlement
to the old village, and the dwarfs visited the latter
place and brought away all the timber, furniture, tools,
cooking utensils. and whatever else they could make
use of, to add to and improve their new village. Hammawhaxo showed that he had a wise head and a good

heart, as well as an able hand. By his teachings and
by his example he was of great benefit. He labored
hard to build and adorn their houses — he instructed
them and their children in many useful arts — with
the assistance of the American sailors, he built boats
and fishing vessels — in fine, he was constantly helping others, and teaching them to help themselves. A
spirit of industry, contentment, and mutual good will
seemed to pervade the little village. Things were
going on so well, that when Mr. Nabbum and Jacky
left, they felt no anxiety about their future success.

After a stay of several months, during which time
Mr. Nabbum had ample opportunity to make many
valuable acquisitions to the great Huggermugger Museum he has since established in America, they bid an
affectionate farewell to the carpenter and tailor. and
promising to visit them again, if ever they made another
voyage in those seas, they sailed homeward, and reached
the United States in health and safety.

CHAPTER SIXTEEN.

MR. NABBUM'S MUSEUM. CONCLUSION.

NE evening I was sitting alone in my study, thinking what sort of a story I should write for my young friends' next Christmas present. I scratched my head, and bit my pen, and poked the fire, and looked into it — then I stood up and gave myself a good warming — then I sat down with my head on my hand, and a blank quire of paper before me — then I took my pen and began to scribble imps — then I became very sleepy — when there was a knock at my door, and to my great surprise in came Jacky Cable. I didn't know him at first, with his bronzed face, his great beard, and his broad shoulders. He had just

arrived from the East Indies, and from Hugger-mugger's Island. So, after a hearty greeting and a warm
welcome, he took a chair by my fire, where he sat
steadily talking and telling stories till—will you believe
it?—two o'clock in the morning.

So I decided to make a book out of what he told
me—and here you have it.

But I have one thing more to tell. I thought I had
got through with my story, and the other day was
just writing the last page, when Mr. Zebedee Nabbum
came stalking in in a state of great excitement.

"If you are reelly goin' to make a book out of
what Jacky's told you," said he, "don't do it—till
you've seen my museum—because I want you to
bring it in somehow."

"Dear me," I said, "I have just got through. I'm
afraid it's too late. My story is all written, and must
go to be printed."

"No, it aint too late," said Zebedee; "you can
tech in a leetle here and there, like—you know—jest
as a kind of seasonin' or sharp *sarce*, to give it a
flavor—can't you? Why, you'd ought to see my
museum, reely. Jacky told you about it, didn't he?"

I said, "Yes, Jacky mentioned that you intended to

set up a museum, a great deal better than Barnum's, and had brought home many curious things from the giant's island."

" *Haint* I though!" said Nabbum. " Why you can't do the subject jestice, till you've seen the things I've got. You must come and see. It dooz beat all nater. Why the few privileged persons that's seen it *do* say that it's no mistake—the most remarkable collection of nateral curiosities that was ever got up in the States."

I promised Mr. Nabbum that I would certainly give him a call — but repeated that I was now writing the last chapter of my book, and didn't wish to clog the story with any superfluous details, and " besides," I said, " your museum will be so well known before my book is out, that my notice of it will be useless."

" Well," said Zebedee, " won't you jest run your eye over this list of articles, and bring in some of 'em at the end of your story."

So saying, he handed me a piece of paper, a good deal worn by being carried in the pocket, with some writing on it in pencil.

" They aint all from the giant's island. the things I've put into the Huggermugger Museum," said Zebedee, " but you'll see that some of 'em are."

So I took the list and read it over, and here is an extract from it : —

Three mammoth Pumpkins, with hair growing on them ; each measuring —— feet diameter, and weighing —— tons. (The figures are not legible.)

One Bullfrog Skin : brilliant green : 6 × 4 feet.

Six splendid gigantic Conch Shells. (Figures effaced, but probably of preposterous dimensions.)

One Saucepan — about the size of a large wash-tub — from the giant's house.

One pair Giant's Boots.

Mrs. Huggermugger's Thimble, Scissors, &c.

One Bottle, with the Cork that killed forty dwarfs.

One rare Bird, stuffed, of stupendous size ; commonly called the Black-Tooter, or Pulpit-Bird. It had a remarkably loud voice.

One specimen of the Musical Crab, found on the shores of Cape Horn.

One curious specimen of Crinoline Petticoat, supposed, from its extraordinary diameter, to have been worn by a giantess.

A winged White Bear, from Iceland. This singular creature was caught on Mount Hecla, where a flock of them were seen fluttering around the burning crater of the volcano, like moths around a candle.

A Salamander. This animal was also caught on Mount Hecla. The end of his tail was seen sticking out of the crater. It took fifty Norwegian sailors to capture him.

A Sea Serpent, larger than any yet seen. This animal had swallowed a meeting-house on Cape Cod, and died of indigestion.

A Daguerreotype of the Emperor of Japan, and a Model of the last Earthquake in that island.

One petrified Monkey.

Two Ducks, born without legs.

One very remarkable Centipede, with eyes in its tail.

One dried Mannikin, preserved in spirits; supposed by Z. N. to be Kobboltozo.

And so on, and so on.

"Well, Mr. Nabbum," I said, after I had ran over the list, "since you have done me such a service in furnishing so much of the material of my story, I will publish the account of our conversation, and a list of some of these wonderful curiosities."

And now I say to all my young readers, after you have read my story, go and see the Huggermugger Museum —— if you can find it.

www.ingramcontent.com/pod-product-compliance
Lightning Source LLC
Chambersburg PA
CBHW032202010726
47493CB00008BA/2796